you matter

christian robinson

SIMON & SCHUSTER

London New York Sydney Toronto New Delhi

The small stuff too small to see.

Those who swim with the tide

and those who don't.

The first to go and the last.

You matter.

When everyone thinks you're a pest.

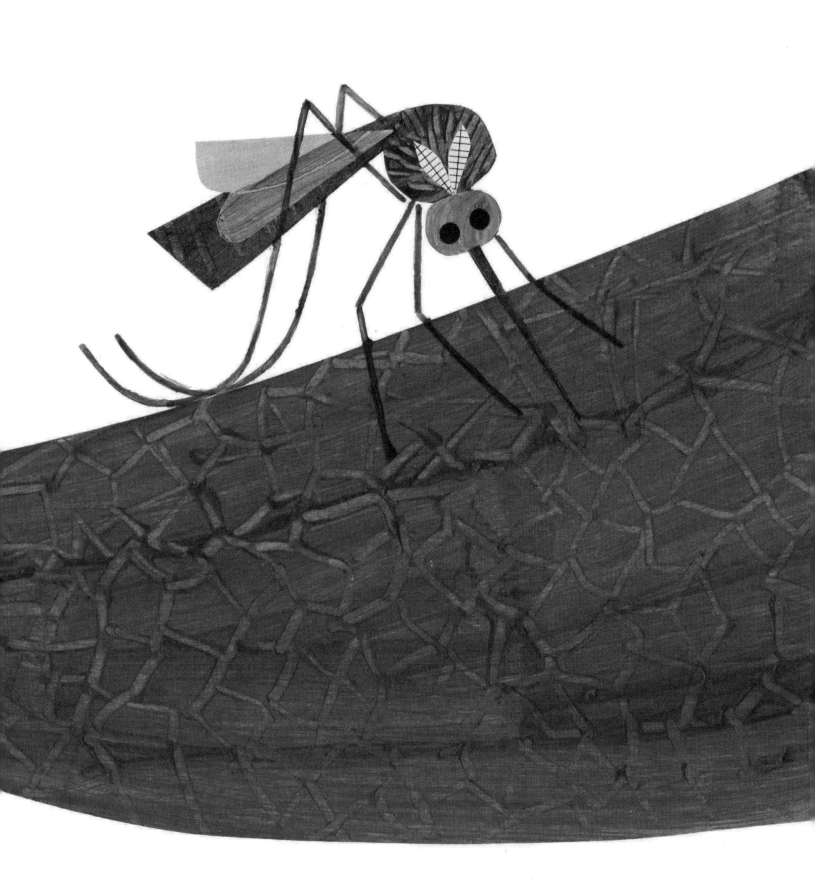

When something is just out of reach.

When everyone is too busy to help.

You matter.

If you fall down.

If you have to start all over again.

Even if you are really gassy.

You matter.

Sometimes home is far away.

Sometimes someone you love says goodbye.

Sometimes you feel lost and alone.

But you matter.

Old and young.

The first to go and the last.

The small stuff too small to see.

You matter.